INKSTAINS

JOHN URBANCIK

CARNIVAL AND CIRCUS

InkStains: Series 2
January

Carnival and Circus

John Urbancik

For more information, please visit www.darkfluidity.com

ISBN-10: 0-9983882-1-1
ISBN-13: 978-0-9983882-1-2 (DarkFluidity)

For every dreamer
ever interrupted
who returned to bed
with hope.

ACKNOWLEDGMENTS

It would've been impossible to write all these stories by hand without the help of numerous fountain pens and an ever-changing assortment of inks. I used Lechtturm1917 notepads this year, despite that they have provided me with no promotional considerations.

As I took this journey, Mery-et suffered the most as she gave me her full support. Thank you.

And thanks, as always, to Sabine and the Rose Fairy.

INKSTAINS

JOHN URBANCIK

CARNIVAL AND CIRCUS

INTRODUCTION

With the first InkStains project, which I began on 1 January 2013, I wrote a story every day for a year. By hand. I allowed one day off per month.

On 1 January 2014, my hand rested, and it was grateful.

Before the year ended, I knew I would do it again, but I wondered: what could I do to differentiate the second series from the first?

Themes.

Monthly themes, to which I stuck – for good or ill.

As with the first set, all genres and styles and types of written work was available to me – unless the theme prescribed restrictions.

The themes forced me to go through the obvious and familiar until I could find the wonderful and absurd.

These are the results: regardless of success or failure. I made zero editorial decisions as to what to include. After typing the stories, I cleaned up grammar and spelling; I did my best to strengthen the writing where it was weak. I'm very happy with a lot of the stories, and disappointed with others, but I think some are fantastic. (I'm biased. You decide.)

So again, please, I invite you to follow me on this journey. See where I went, what I was thinking, and what influenced me.

As you read this year's writing, I'm doing it a third time. I've embarked on yet another InkStains project, with a different approach to monthly themes.

JANUARY

Carnival and Circus.

It's a broad theme, one that's been visited innumerable times by writers with great talent, great ambition, both, or neither.

I had to get used to writing complete stories daily again. I had to familiarize myself with the pace, with the structures, with the overall demand. I stumbled once or twice, but I think, in the end, I found my way.

1 JANUARY

A cold breeze makes its way through the carnival's skeleton. It passes rusted structures with faded names; rides that will never move again; stands that, once upon a time, sold fairy floss and funnel cakes; and ivy-bound tracks from the roller coasters. The breeze tugs at posters made illegible by the constant sun. It swirls around pins waiting to be knocked over, and climbs to the bell at the top of a strongman tower. A discarded mallet sits at the base of that unsteady tower.

The breeze pulls only a thin, hollow peal from the bell, but it's an uncommon enough sound in this forsaken meadow to attract attention.

A bird arrives first, a brilliant red cardinal. He lands on the bell itself, then alights and settles on the handle of the mallet.

Another bird, a woodpecker, though she cannot possibly find food within, strikes the bell with her beak. The sound is stronger, more resonant, and it echoes beyond the boundaries of the creaking, oxidized meadow.

Field mice and squirrels and voles and marmots come to explore, and behind them the predators: feral cats, foxes, coyotes, even the wolves, until finally a man – something very like a man – strides out of the woods.

He is broad as an ox and just as tough and just as strong, and he wears the ancient garb of woodsmen. He marvels aloud as he follows the breeze's path through the dilapidation. "I used to come to such fairs as a child," he says to no one. "I would bob for apples and ride the carousel and test my strength."

Just then, he comes upon the high striker, the tarnished bell at its peak, the mallet trembling in anticipation. He lifts it, and it seems small in his hands. He tests its weight, tosses it from right to left, and says, "As a child, I never could ring that bell."

He is a particularly strong man, if older than he appears. He is healthy and hale and of good stock. He raises the mallet over his head and swings down. The chaser, which hasn't stirred in ages – decades, at least, perhaps centuries – races toward the bell. But it falls just short, missing by an inch, maybe less.

The broad woodsman swings again. And again. He works up a sweat and a burn in his muscles, but the chaser never fails to miss its mark.

"Maybe there's something stuck up there," he says.

"I don't think that's it at all." The woman sits on the edge of an unrecognizable ride. She may have been watching him a long time. She wears a sundress the color of dawn and her lustrous blonde hair would compete with diamonds in its vibrance. She hops off the ride and approaches, then holds out a hand for the mallet.

He hands it over and steps aside. "You may be the stronger," he admits, though of course he suspects this is not the truth. She is beauty and grace, not iron, and not brick. He can see the effort she expends to carry the heavy mallet.

"Oh, no," she says, stepping on a board at the base of the tower to depress a hidden lever that tightens the wire the chaser climbs. "I merely have a better understanding of tension."

With one easy swing, she sends the chaser up to the bell, which rings brilliantly. She grins and gives him back the mallet and says, "I just rang your bell."

John Urbancik

2 JANUARY

You would think the rides themselves are alive, and that their ghosts linger even after the carnival has packed up and shipped out. The field seems barren, but you can still hear children laughing and the noise of diving pigs and the echo of tinny, pre-recorded pipe organs. You smell all the sugar and the sweat. You feel your heart pounding in the haunted maze and see yourself distorted in smudged mirrors.

Yes, if you squat just right, looking toward the sun, you can see tents and carousels.

It is, after all, twilight, a magical time, the tenuous barrier between day and night. In that yellow-tinged light, all things are possible. Apples can be candied. Clowns shot full of water. Unicorns brought to life.

The trash is definitely real, no mere imagination figment. Discarded bags of popcorn and peanuts dance in the wind. Posters linger on street posts and trees. The moon, a pale shade not unlike a clown's make-up, glows dimly as a prelude to the stars.

And yes, of course, in the moon you find a witness. Like you, she saw the carnival in this field; and like you, she sees it still, though she also sees its trucks parked in some far away meadow where they're preparing to open in another town and inspire another dream.

The moon shared in all your glories, did she not?

You bend a knee and touch the ground and still feel the thunder of footsteps and carousel horses. Their spirits threaten to steal you away. There are far away meadows and fields, towns with names you'll never be able to pronounce, romances to kindle and fancies to ignite. Maybe you, like the carnival, are meant for the road. Sedentary life is boring. There are foods you've never eaten, and musicians you've never heard play. There are clouds in shapes you've never expected. Maybe you, like the carnival, can seek out other horizons. Pack up everything you are, leave only traces behind, traces and memories, and find a new adventure every night.

Maybe you, like the carnival, can find guidance in the moon. She's something of a god. She'll light your path. Protect you from all the faces of evil. Keep you cool on those hot summer nights.

Maybe you, like the carnival, should leave this place, this town and this meadow, this particular life.

Maybe you, like the carnival, are merely a lingering ghost.

3 JANUARY

The city is dense, filled with bricks and iron and asphalt, concrete and glass towers that cut the sky, but sometimes – when the sky has been gray for days on end, when summer isn't living up to its promise of warmth and fun – you have to escape the oppression of the city and find a bit of space.

The city is surrounded by wide open spaces. Suburbs. Farms. Beaches. Meadows. Jill takes her friend Jack, who has a car, and they flee the city in search of mischief and fattening foods and games of chance.

In short, they seek a fair.

In summers, the televisions shows are filled with ads for country fairs and Nathan's hot dog eating contests and various temporary amusements. Just take this highway ten, twenty miles out of the city – east, west, north, it doesn't matter.

They drive east first, through a tunnel and its wide expanses of interstate. It's early in the day, still gray even so far from the city, and when they get off the highway they stop for a breakfast of peanut butter and chocolate muffins and orange juice. They find entire subdivisions consisting of only a single house color and three different shapes. They find the ghosts of strip malls. Vacant lots. Great big malls that sell jewelry and coats and paper weights and sunglasses.

They find no fair, no signs pointing to a fair, no meadows large enough to host a fair.

"We should go north instead," Jill suggests as Jack refills the gas tank. "Into the mountains."

Half an hour later they cross a bridge and venture north, beyond railroad graveyards and handball courts, into streets that wind not just right and left but up and down. You could almost believe there's no such thing as a city when there are so many trees. They cross countless streams and rivers. They drive past centuries-old courthouses and public squares. They stop for lunch in an Italian place, they meander through florist shops and bookstores, they stop at a great big utilitarian library and, at the reference desk, ask for information about the fair.

It's ten minutes of work. The librarian checks the internet, cross-references her sources, and even makes a phone call in which she actually talks to someone, before stating, "The fair left town a week ago Saturday." Before Jill can ask the next obvious question, the librarian answers it: "Apparently, they're headed next for someplace in Delaware."

It almost doesn't matter what city you call home; Delaware seems dreadfully far away, and Jack's already got to refuel the car again.

They do a bit of walking around a lake. They share some chocolate. Jack buys Jill a single red rose before they get back to his car.

"No fair," Jack said.

"No," Jill agrees. "It's not fair."

Worse, the sky is still gray, the promised summer heat still unrealized, and the day is already transitioning to night.

They return to the city, to the endless rows of boulevards and avenues, to the millions of people, to the asphalt and steel under gray, gray skies. They're disappointed, yes, but it was a good day out by any measure, and even if they found no fair, they'd escaped the city.

They go to a fancy expensive trendy place for dinner, where the dishes are huge and the portions indescribably small but the flavors exquisite. Briefly, Jill thinks she can taste the rural air in her meal, and the wine is wonderful.

It was an early dinner, and it seems now the day has come to an end. You cannot see the gray in the sky, only the infinite twinkling of city lights like stars, and brake lights like fireworks, and mobile phones like will-o-the-wisps blinking on and off in the city streets.

Neither wants the day to end. Not here. Not yet. So they walk some, through the city in the early evening, and they come upon a bar they've never seen. Snippets of jazz escape every time the door swings open.

"Should we?" Jack asks.

The name of the place is written on the door: *The Carnival.* They take it as a sign.

4 JANUARY

Life is a carnival.

There are thrill rides, roller-coasters and haunted houses, the events that get out hearts pumping and adrenaline active. We go from ride to ride on a daily basis, not just when we're in cars and subways and those metallic tubes hurling at impossible speeds through the sky. Not just the elevators which might stop between floors or the freezer doors that might slam shut on your fingers. We face excitement – or we opt to avoid uncertainty – with almost every breath – or we revel and/or cower in the consequences.

There are games of chance. Some might say they're games of skill. They may be rigged so the odds are against you. (It's often hard to remember that sometimes life is unfair in your advantage.) We don't always know what we'll face, but with risk comes rewards. Sure, sometimes that reward is merely a tiny stuffed koala that feels more like a bean bag. (Here's a life hint: win three of those, then you can juggle!)

There's food. There's lots of food. Good food, bad food, foods you like and foods you hate. (Another life hint, in the form of a question: haven't you had enough food? Or: isn't there enough for everyone?)

There are sword swallowers and fire breathers and bearded women and contortionists all over the place. Maybe you should redefine what you think of as Freaks. Because there are also math wizards, mixologists, quarterbacks, and soccer moms – all manner of madmen, poets, and thieves – accomplishing things today that you find impossible.

Because all kinds of things are impossible. Yet here we are, in this carnival of life, standing atop our personal diving platform over minuscule washbasins filled with sudsy water. We – you and I and everybody – daily stand against the impossible on a tiny blue sphere spinning around a persistent thermonuclear reaction on the outskirts of a galaxy so wide it must be measured in relative abstractions. We stand against the impossible surrounded by whirling lights and screaming children and vibrant colors and aromas and every imaginable and unimaginable distraction. We stand against the impossible and we hand over our money. We buy our tickets for the carnival. We ride the rides. We defy doubt and fear and obstruction every day, even on the worst of our days.

And on our best days? We build carnivals.

5 JANUARY

The old man enters the coffee shop followed by a strong gust of chilled wind before the door bangs shut behind him. He pauses there, perhaps accustomed to making an entrance. He's of a stocky build, still strong – not frail or withered, but well-weathered, a face pocked by miniscule scars that combine to make something of a texture. His eyes are sharp, crystalline even, and though they don't dart swiftly about, they seem to see everything in amazing detail.

The moment of his entrance behind him, he strides to the counter and orders a chocolate from the pretty girl with spider web tattoos in the web of her thumb and fingers.

It's a cold winter, with snow and ice and negative degrees; everything and everyone seems grayed and muted, even the fashionable ladies in their black – the newest black – and their colorful designer clutches.

The old man takes a seat alone at a table near the restroom. He doesn't huddle to gather or reclaim warmth. He removes his heavy jacket to reveal autumn colors, solid muscles, a breath of fresh cider and maple.

A girl with a camera asks if she can take his picture for a website. It's for a school project. He agrees, but he doesn't smile for the shot. It wouldn't be entirely natural.

Another college kid, this one scrawny, a man who hasn't yet earned the title, who has never had to work with his hands, approaches timidly and says, "I'm writing an essay. For school."

With a wave of his hand, the old man invites him to sit. "I ain't much of a writer myself. How can I help?"

The girl with the spider tattoo brings his chocolate and a bit of a smile. He thanks her.

The college kid says, "I'm supposed to write a story – an essay – about something from the past. Anything. I'm supposed to interview my father or grandfather or..." He hesitates.

"I may be older than I look," the old man tells him, skipping the part where the kid has to admit an uncomfortable truth about his father or grandfather.

"Could I maybe ask you some questions?"

The old man nods, buy says, "You've been asking questions, but I can't say you've asked anything of substance." He sips his chocolate.

"I hope to," the kid says. "Can I start with your name?"

"No," the old man says. "That's a terrible place to start. What good is my name? What does that tell you about me?"

"It tells me what to call you."

The old man shakes his head. "Maybe I should ask the questions. What is it you want to know? Did I place stickball? Was I in a gang? The theater? Have I killed a man? Did I enjoy it? Would I do it again? What about love? Is it worth it, all the trouble and the damn drama, the insincerity, the mystery of it all? Maybe you want to know about the first time I kissed a girl. Or robbed a bank. Maybe you want to know about my seventeenth summer. I was younger than you, then, and I learned something important. Something unforgettable." He paused to sip his chocolate.

"That," the kid finally says. "The summer story."

The old man glances out the window. "I guess we all could use a bit of warmth. Okay, fine, I'll share my seventeenth summer. It was a magical time. There was a girl, of course – and as I said, there was murder. It must've been sixty years ago. More." He leaned forward to confide, "It wasn't the first time I was seventeen."

The kid blinked. "What?"

The old man grabbed his hand and said, with complete sincerity, "Some stories are best experienced."

Then the coffee shop was gone, at least for the college kid. Gone, too, was winter, all the snow and ice and cold. He found himself instead at the back entrance of a country fair. He wasn't himself.

"Sit back," the old man said, a voice in his head. "These are just memories, and some of them might even be true."

Then the college kid, helpless to resist, strode into the fair where the young man worked, and he proceeded to learn something important – something unforgettable.

6 JANUARY

Long ago, in the early days, before people even walked the earth, there were gods – or something like gods – for all the things. Every mountain had its god, and every tree in the forest. Every boulder had a god, and every star in the sky.

The gods and goddesses often bickered and often fought and often loved one another with reckless abandon. And sometimes – in fact, with great frequency – gods died. Trees are devastated by forest fires. Lightning only lasts for a very short time, so its gods, feisty as they may be, were short-lived. Cloud gods had interesting habits in the sky. Gods of constellations might think themselves better than all the individual stars. The god of the sun claims to be the oldest, most powerful god on earth.

In comparison, the gods of the internet are young, as are the gods of automobiles and gold coins and fountain pens. A great many gods, in fact, were brought into existence by the fancies and ingenuity of mankind – who, perhaps, could lay claim to the title, "God of Gods," as they're always so busy creating new ones. Every iPod had its own god. Every pair of denim jeans. Every horse on every carousel at every carnival.

Indeed, on any given night, after the carnival lights have gone out and the carnies are busy in their beds, when the children are dreaming of the fantastic sights they've only just beheld, the gods of the carnival crawl out of their cubbyholes and gather for their own entertainments.

You may find the thrill ride gods, no longer spinning and whirling and tilting and plunging from dizzying heights, sharing brandy and discussing Shakespeare. Some of the gods from games of chance might be playing dice. A god from the rope climb and a goddess from the Ferris wheel might find themselves, limbs all entwined, behind a fence near the ticket booth.

The truth is, the gods of the carnival, like all the little gods, want the same kinds of things we – the little humans – desire. So when we're there, eating fairy floss and getting our weights guessed, it might be a good idea to say thank you to the god of the clown face you're shooting full of water. You might praise the god of that ring you're tossing. You might even love the goddess of the carousel's lead horse. You never know when they might be feeling generous.

7 JANUARY

So very cold.

The walls are glass. Or ice – it's impossible to know. Jill runs between them, turning left and right, discovers another distorted image of herself. Fat. Tall. Scarred. Frozen blue.

From somewhere, he laughs.

She runs into a transparent wall. Bangs her head. It hurts. She doesn't even see a hint of her reflection in it, no glimmer or light, no hope of escape.

Somewhere behind her, another panel of glass shatters. She has to keep moving. Her heart races. Her breaths burst out in icy plumes. She can almost imagine herself as an ice dragon, pure white under a frozen sea in the Antarctic.

She'd be more comfortable there.

Another glass wall shatters. She sees it break in another distorting mirror, as though a thousand sheets of glass shatter at once.

Stop panicking, she tells herself. Concentrate. Think. Make deliberate choices. Act with reason and intention. Ignore his incessant cackling. Picture that dragon again, rising from the funhouse maze, consuming the man who thinks he's a god in a single bite.

You're a dragon, she tells herself. Dragons devour little godlings.

Another turn, three steps forward: dead end. Mirror to the left of her. Mirror to the right. Infinite Jill's reaching to the beginning and the end of time. Glass or ice in front of her, frozen solid, stealing the warmth from her hand as she touches it, leans against it, slumps into it.

Jill turns, but there's no place left to run. He's right there, Jack, the grinning self-proclaimed evil master of mazes and mirrors, awakened to godlike potential.

Jill gasps for breath. It's like getting punched in the stomach. The cold hurts her skin.

But she's not alone. To the left of her, and to the right, stand another Jill, and another next to them – a thousand and a million and more – twin abysses of Jill's.

She inhales deeply, despite the cold that tears her throat, and draws all those other Jill's into her, increasing her strength logarithmically, until she can hardly contain herself. More than that.

She grows. She expands. She shatters the glass walls and the mirrors and the maze – all the things over which Jack has dominion. Her armored tail stretches behind her like a river of white.

Jill spreads her wings and rises over the entire ice carnival. It's hers, this place – not just the maze which is nothing but shards of glass – but every spindly spire, every statue, every icicle. She is the ice dragon now, and when she opens her mouth to scream the roar shakes the moon frozen in its place in the sky.

Jack stands there, ready to challenge her, all confident in his godly abilities. She swallows him whole.

It's a dream, of course, all a mist within her head, the images already scattering as she wakes. But she wakes with indigestion, and there's no sign of Jack in the apartment they share, and the winter air feels unusually comfortable.

John Urbancik

8 JANUARY

On a seemingly random Thursday, when the moon was neither full nor new, when there was no particularly notable storm crackling overhead, on the sidewalk of an ordinary boring street downtown, as she hurried to the bus stop from a mundane day job, Jill stepped on a crack in the cement.

It was a fresh, twisting crack, still forming, still expanding, and it was just big enough to swallow Jill whole.

She disappeared – not just from the street, not merely from the city, but from the face of the earth. Most of the rest of the world went on doing all the things they'd been doing. And though a great many people noticed her absence, and even sought explanations, it was an extraordinarily small fraction of a single percent of the people, not merely in the world but in that single city and on that single street, that noticed when she vanished.

Jill, meanwhile, noticed immediately, as you might expect. One moment, the world around her was a city with city sounds – automobile horns and tires and the breathing of buildings and the thump of eight million hearts – and the next, she was on a carnival midway surrounded by cheaply made signs and the overwhelming scents of caramel apples and livestock.

It was all very disconcerting, especially since her plans for the evening had involved wine and fancy dinner plates and a gentleman friend her co-workers had been trying to set her up with for months – not a spinning, whirling machine whose gears clicked almost as loudly as the music meant to drown it out.

There were, of course, other rides, and an assortment of games – basketballs and plastic horses and rope and the like – and a variety of deep-fried culinary options she'd never considered.

The carnival was crowded. Packed. Dense as any city street. But the streets carving their way between attractions were dirt. And the cacophony of heartbeats raced so much more swiftly.

The sun was low, not quite yet setting; if she could've seen the sun through the city, it may have been at the same angle and intensity. Here, it felt hotter. More vibrant. More real.

It couldn't be real. That was a given. Jill assumed she was destined for a date with a pharmacological buffet. Anti-anxiety, anti-depressant, anti-psychotic – anti-life pills in a rainbow of colors.

A man approached her through the crowd. He wasn't just a random guy walking in her direction who would continue past. He came straight to her. He stopped in front of her and smiled.

It was, she had to admit, a gorgeous smile.

"Jill," he said, shoving a hand forward to shake hello. "So pleased to finally meet you." He held her hand a moment without a single overly exuberant pump, and he let go before it became awkward. "I thought maybe to surprise you. Dinner can be so over-rated and dull."

"Jack?" she asked.

"I hope they only said good things about me," he said, "because I would've paid them to lie if I'd thought about it."

"Where are we?"

He smiled again, though he had never really stopped. "The carnival, of course."

Of course. She blinked. She smiled; she couldn't resist. She asked, "But what are we doing here?"

"We," Jack said, offering an arm in an old-fashioned gentlemanly way, "are going on a date."

And it was a spectacular date. Jill was home by morning.

John Urbancik

9 JANUARY

Posters went up three weeks ahead of time. "Travelling Carnival," they announced, with a date and place, and nothing more than the barest, most simplistic graphic: minimalism at its finest, a single line curved to represent the sun-drenched edge of a tent.

"Travelling Carnival" wasn't much of a description. But like the line indicating a tent filled with tigers and jugglers and magicians, the two words were wonderfully evocative. The choice of typeface was exquisite, obviously, because by the end of the first weekend after the posters started appearing, no one seemed capable of talking about anything else.

There were all the regular questions, of course. Whose carnival was coming? Would they have acrobats? Fire breathers? Everybody expected fire breathers. How could they possibly stock enough hot dogs and lemons for lemonade?

Under normal circumstances, children dreamed of running away to join a circus. But for this brief time, it was a carnie's life they sought. On the road. One with the dust and the sun. Winks for all the pretty ladies.

The night before the Travelling Carnival was set to arrive, the appointed field was barren, devoid of any sign of mirth or merriment. One could scarcely believe what it would transform into overnight. A train would arrive, or a series of trucks, with rides and freaks and spectacular exhibits of Egyptian mummies and spices from the Far East.

Jack, for one – and he wasn't alone – had difficulty sleeping. It was like Christmas Eve in the middle of summer. He dreamt of bizarre things: hippopotamuses swimming in aquariums, ropes climbing the air in perfect rhythm to old wooden flutes. In the morning, his mom made him eat breakfast – a whole breakfast, with eggs and sausage links. And she made him drink an entire glass of orange juice because it just wouldn't do to experience an insufficiency of Vitamin C. It wouldn't do at all.

Finally, Jack was released. He raced across town to the great big field that should've been filled with rodeo clowns and sheep ready for sheering and flashing lights and conmen.

There certainly was a crowd.

But a carnival? Jack saw no sign of any such thing. No slides, no horses, no apple carts or gypsy girls.

There was a tent. In the center of the field, seemingly surrounded by the entire town, stood a single olive green tent. It was small, neither long enough nor wide enough to hold more than a single person, though it was tall enough that he could sit upon one of two plain wood stools beside a single uninspiring table. It might've been a TV tray, fit for a bowl of mac and cheese and a Pepsi. Three sides of the square tent were down, one side open to reveal the unassuming gentleman.

Yet the crowd pressed close, a crowd filled with other kids and teenagers and grown-ups and slow-moving old men. The crowd was loud, so that no single voice could be understood in the din. Many clutched dollars in their hands.

While Jack watched, men and women of all sizes, shapes, and colors made their way closer to the tent. There seemed to be no order, no actual line, no indication of a wait time – or, indeed, of what they were waiting for. Some people seemed to circle the tent, getting no closer to handing over their dollar. The dollars themselves seemed to vanish once they got inside the little tent.

A surge of disappointment drove Jack forward, through the crowd, right up to the very edge of the tent. There, he watched a woman as old as his schoolteacher enter the tent. She gave the man her dollar. He whispered something in her ear. She blushed. She smiled. She left.

Then a teenager got in. He seemed to hold his dollar like a cruel prankster training a kitten. They exchanged words until, reluctantly, the teenager handed over his dollar. The man smiled, leaned closer and whispered something, then leaned back. The teenager remained seated for a full minute at least. He blinked no less than twice, then eventually remembered where he was, got off the stool, and merged into the crowd.

"Go on," someone said, pushing Jack forward. "It's your turn."

Then Jack was in the tent. It seemed to dull the noise from outside. He approached the empty stool tentatively. The man smiled at him.

"I don't understand," Jack said. "Where's the carnival?"

"It's all an illusion," the man said. "I pared it down to its most basic elements."

"What do I get for my dollar?" Jack asked.

"Nothing but the truth."

Jack glanced behind him and outside the tent. A lot of people strained to see more clearly or maybe catch a hint of what the man might say. He pulled a crumpled dollar out of his pocket and gave it to the man. "Thank you," the man said.

Jack did not see where the dollar disappeared to.

The man leaned closer and whispered, "It's all a trick. There is no carnival. But I bet, if you don't tell anyone what I've said, a thousand people will give me their dollar today, and another thousand tomorrow."

"I don't believe it," Jack said.

"It's true."

"What if I do tell?"

"You may," the man said, "but no one will believe you, and they'll want to hear the truth for themselves. As it is, you're in on my little secret, Jack, and that makes you special."

Bewildered, and perhaps shocked, Jack left the tent. It was only later that he wondered how the man had known his name.

10 JANUARY

Outside, they dance. They wear less clothing than is possible, drink more beer than is likely, and blast whatever music they can find at a level for which the speakers are woefully ill-prepared.

They don't even know what they celebrate or why, but they don't care. There are no bad reasons for a party, especially one that encompasses entire cities and countrysides.

Outside, they dance; but inside, all the sounds are muted by somber walls, the air is heavy with layers of stale incense and cigarettes, and an unhealthy quantity of bourbon remains untouched.

The girl lies in bed, watched over and protected, prayed for, loved. She whispers sometimes, but no longer seems capable of speech. They keep cold white towels by her bedside to sop up the sweat. She is, basically, dead, though her heart hasn't quite realized it. The rhythm of her life persists. She lingers. The ghost of her remains trapped within her bones and blood. She is beyond hope, if not beyond pain. If there's any sort of mercy, then perhaps she is no longer conscious.

She's far too young for all the color to have seeped from her flesh. She hasn't yet earned a wrinkle. She hasn't had children. She's not yet had time to write the adventures of her life. She hasn't had to decide upon any paths. All her options have been removed.

Her mother touches her cheek, says, "She's burning," and cries. She cries a lot. The rest of the family tries to keep her away, but she is drawn to her daughter – her baby – as any mother would be.

Her father stares at a glass of bourbon. He's been carrying that same tumbler for weeks. There's never been any need to refill it; he knows what he'll become if he submits, and he's been at least strong enough to deny that.

Her sister stares out the window of an upstairs bedroom. From there, one can see the celebration, but her sister sees instead beyond the lights to the city of the dead, the crosses and mausoleums, the resting corpses inside their marble homes.

Her brother sits by her side and, when he kneels to pray, asks that she be released. He also sneaks out of the house at night and gives urchins small amounts of money to run about the fete and acquire certain promises and favors. As yet, his efforts have been unrewarded, and he despairs of the current circumstances ever changing.

Near midnight on the last night of the celebration, as she tosses in bed and cries out and burns, there is a knock on the door.

The visitor does not wait for the door to be opened, but enters. No one thinks to stop him. He wears make-up to accentuate the bones of his skull. He walks straight to her bedroom and raises a hand and says some words in French or Creole.

Another visitor, an inhumanly tall and thin woman, arrives as he leaves. She touches the girl's forehead, nearly pulling her fingers away from the heat, then bends over to leave a kiss there.

Twin boys arrive next. They flank the girl in her bed but don't seem to do or say anything.

An old lady comes with a bowl of soup, which she leaves on the girl's bedside table.

A ghost visits, then a Shadow Man, a doctor, a witchdoctor, and a priest of some sort. Twin priestesses of an underground sex cult perform a brief ceremony. A child brings a lily. A poetess brings words, and a glass blower leaves an offering of fragrant smoke.

The prince arrives just before the midnight hour. Outside, they dance. The prince would also dance. There is reason to celebrate. He says to the girl, "Dance with me," and for the first time in a long time she opens her eyes and casts off her bedsheets. Against all probability, she dances with the prince. A waltz. It's quite a thing to see.

As the clock prepares to signal the day's end, he whispers to her, "You may kiss me, if you wish."

The girl's mother cries when a prince of death makes such an offer to her daughter. The girl says, "Thank you, but I'm not ready yet."

The prince smiles. He leads her back to the bed. Her fever has returned and she subsides back to a restless non-death.

The prince makes his bows and leaves.

Outside, they no longer dance. Midnight has passed. The music has ceased. The celebration is ended.

Inside, the girl's fever breaks. At dawn, she wakes and asks for water. Her mother cries that it's a miracle. Her father thanks all the gods, no matter how big or small. Her sister stops staring at the cemeteries and finds a good, restful sleep. And her brother begins the work of paying off his debt.

11 JANUARY

Many years ago, in what seemed to be a random field, a man who ran a travelling carnival decided he was done with life on the road. So, when the carnival set up shop, they left the road.

No one objected.

Over time, the temporary tents were replaced with constructed frames, which were later replaced with magical replicas filled with swirls of color and bizarre statuary.

The carousel shifted a few feet to the west and sent its roots deep into the earth. Then it grew, adding height and depth and, at first, an entire row of houses – then another.

Games of chance were gradually replaced by shows, demonstrations, and souvenir kiosks.

The man, formerly the first truck driver, owner, manager, and master of ceremonies, became something of a businessman. He ran two types of amusement parks, one on top of the other. You might find fairy floss at one of the food carts, but you might also find faerie dust, which was something else entirely. Certain services were available from some of the performers if you knew how to ask. Security men were also bouncers for the burlesque shows and leg-breakers when required.

A castle grew in the center of the park. It seemed appropriate, but it became the haunted house, and it seemed to be haunted primarily by the ghosts of people who'd lost their innocence in the park at night.

Every summer, a boy disappeared. People thought there was a jilted lover seeking vengeance, but could never agree on the details of her story. Was she old or young? Angry or heartbroken? A park employee?

In the height of a real estate boom, a roller coaster was built. It circled the entire park and ran for almost eight minutes. It was a wooden coaster, and though it was originally called The Snake, it later became The Spider Dragon, though it stole this name from another carnival that still travelled.

One year, heavy rains brought floods and the park was damaged. The next year, a gang war ended, with an extraordinary amount of bloodshed, in the park the same summer night the boy disappeared. The year after: murder. The businessman was found dead, poisoned, in one of the brothels. It was blamed on the whiskey, or the whiskey glass, and his murderer was never caught.

After he died, the decay accumulated.

A rash of food poisoning was blamed on the bakery. The popularity of faerie dust waned in favor of more exotic chemical concoctions. The burlesque's prima donna's affair with a rich suitor ended in suicide. The carnival horses began to grow sick and wander off to die in peace. The statues melted or fell or evaporated.

The roller coaster stopped rolling. Ivy consumed its architecture and, in seemingly no time at all, consumed the entire thing. The frames of the most basic buildings withered into dust.

In the end, the field became home to a series of tents and games of change. One random Monday morning, the carnival packed up and moved on with a new ringleader.

John Urbancik

12 JANUARY

The circus is coming.

There's still time to pack a bag and get out of town. They've got clowns, after all, and a cannon, and nets like spider webs to ensnare you.

They've got jugglers, and you know well enough, by now, not to trust a juggler.

They've got women riding elephants. They'll charge through the streets like tanks, surrounded by their own cavalry, just to clear the way for the tigers.

I only know they'll arrive by rail, so it's safest to travel away from the tracks. Don't stop for popcorn or peanuts. Don't pick up that cute contortionist hitchhiking on the side of the road. As pleasant a way you imagine she'll kill you, you'll still be dead by the time she's done.

Don't take to the trees or the rooftops thinking you're safe. The aerialists can climb faster than you can, they have perfect balance on the briefest of surfaces, and they fly.

You should just run.

However strong you think you are, you have never met their strongman. However fast you think you are, they have motorcyclists who defy gravity. However smart you think you are, they have a chimpanzee who plays chess as a grandmaster level.

They are fitter than you, and meaner, and they outnumber you. They have knife throwers. They have Siamese twins that were separated at birth yet share a single, sharply focused mind.

And they can smell you.

The circus has a sword swallower and a girl who breathes fire and a boy who doesn't need to breathe at all. They've got at least two people who can catch bullets with their teeth.

They've even got a Props Master who can build absolutely anything.

I was four when the circus came for me. They ripped me from my family, shoved me in a cage, and paraded me – with all their other new captives – before a crowd of twenty thousand in a smoke-filled arena.

The Ringmaster has a list, and you're on it. He's bringing the circus to your hometown with nothing but malicious intent. The circus is coming, so you'd better run. Run fast and far.

We'll be there at dawn.

13 JANUARY

If I told you a man designed a mechanical dragon twenty feet tall that breathed fire, you might think he was a madman bent on world domination, but in fact he was merely a salaried employee doing a job. In the evenings, he dreamt of singing on Broadway in fantastic glittering costumes.

He designed the dragon to be part of a daily parade at an amusement park where visitors from every corner of the globe could be suitably impressed and take selfies with the mechanized beast in the background. Some of those guests dreamed of becoming honest, full-time photographers travelling the world shooting gorgeous models on beaches with names too vowel-heavy to properly pronounce.

Every day, on command, the mechanical dragon strode down the middle of the street and shot plumes of fire into the air in such a way that no tree limbs or building awnings ever caught fire. But the driver dreamt of one day being unleashed outside of the amusement park, perhaps to protect the world from alien invasion but most likely to go wild with wanton destruction and a certain degree of chaos. The fact that he never took the mechanical dragon out of the park either indicated he was not, in fact, a madman at heart – or that he simply lacked the courage of his convictions.

Every day, a girl sighed as she watched the mechanical dragon roll by. She made snickerdoodle cookies and the third best chocolate brownies available anywhere. But she dreamed of being a dragon, of flying free and breaking all the bonds that held her, of hording treasures under a burning volcano, of commanding fear, love, respect, awe, and devotion.

The President of the corporation that owned the company which owned the parks that hired the designer had approved the plans for the mechanical dragon himself. He'd expected it would bring lots of money into the park, positively impacting the bottom line of that company and therefore satisfying the insatiable desire for profit by the corporation's shareholders. He'd never personally visited the park. Nor had he seen the mechanical dragon, not even in pictures; he might not even remember the thing existed or that it breathed real fire or that someone might someday march it down Broadway. He dreamed of being President of an even larger corporation and moving one spot higher on the list of the world's wealthiest.

The mechanical dragon herself, meanwhile, was rather content, and dreamed of chasing butterflies in the park.

14 JANUARY

The old man walks through his father's garden.

His father had been a great man. He'd made a lot of money running a circus back when that was big, big money. He'd amassed something of an art collection, and he'd built a beautiful estate in Florida.

His wasn't, however, the famous name in circuses, and after his father's untimely death, he – now an old man – failed to make it work.

Today, he still lived on the estate, though he could no longer count his age. And though he'd divested himself of most his father's art collection, he'd done so to maintain the estate.

There were, after all, the statues to look after.

He'd been young when the couple had joined the circus. It was some sort of acrobatic bit; that wasn't the part the old man remembered.

The statues didn't move. They didn't seem to move, at least, which was almost the same. The old man knew better.

When they were young, the acrobats were flirtatious and full of zest. They were friends with everyone, they were vigorous and vibrant, they were insatiable in all their appetites. Even when the old man was a child, he knew what that meant.

On a gin-fueled night, maybe an hour before the dawn, the couple met a man at a party who wasn't anymore a man than the old man was himself an acrobat.

"You move so fast," the non-man said. "Like everything else will disappear around you."

"It just might," the boy acrobat said.

"You'll die young," the non-man said.

"If that is our fate," the girl acrobat said, "then we shall die young."

"That hardly seems fair," the non-man said, "as a young death is most certainly your fate."

Later, some said it had been a threat; others said a warning. The truth was, the old man thought, it was something more like a regret.

"I can't change that," the non-man said, "but perhaps I can slow you down a bit. Would that tempt you?"

The acrobats had laughed. They went outside, the three of them and some others, into the garden, where the non-man said, "I must ask for a payment for my services." He shrugged. "It's something of a rule. To do with balance."

"We are mere circus performers," the boy acrobat had said.

"I'm willing to accept a kiss in payment," the non-man said. "From each of you."

Apparently, that had seemed fair.

There'd been much kissing, witnesses said, as well as fondling, groping, all manner of inappropriate folly. And it was impossible to truly say whether the non-man was entirely male throughout the rest of the night.

Then the Florida sun peeked over the horizon. Dawn moved swiftly, just as the acrobats had always moved swiftly. The acrobats, in the day's first light, were kissing each other, and they were slowing down.

Indeed, they slowed nearly to a standstill, frozen in an eternal youth, together and embroiled forever.

The old man came to the garden every few weeks. He could see how the statues – they seemed like statues to everyone else – had continued in their kissing.

As promised, they'd been slowed down, and the world sped past the otherwise oblivious lovers.

The old man was jealous of their long life together.

John Urbancik

15 JANUARY

In a faraway future, but not all that far from here, the grandmaster of one of the greatest galactic carnivals was born. By the time she was a teenager, she'd trained a hundred ape-like creatures to dance ballet. People came from the moons of Saturn to watch her apes twirling on their toe tips, and she'd had a glimpse already of what her destiny must be.

She trained one of the last surviving cybernetic soldiers to ride on the back of a camel – camels, indigenous only to earth, being one the most rarefied creatures in the known stars. There were, at that time, quite a few known stars, several dark stars that were to be avoided because of their greed, and a half dozen classified as Unknowable and, therefore, left to the fancies of science fiction authors.

She hired a daredevil who had made his own shuttle, which was painted red with white racing stripes, to do tricks around one of the dark stars, swinging close as he somersaulted. He seemed not to age at all.

She hitched the earth's moon, long abandoned as barren and wasted, onto the back of a star squid and trained it to create animal-shaped nebulae with its ink ejections.

By the time she was twenty, she'd made a pet of a firefly. In her laboratories, she increased its size – but not its mass – and taught the firefly to light, like a star in the sky, then fall on her travelling carnival so that everyone in the audience would be permitted to make wishes.

Shortly thereafter, she bought out the Trump Traveling Circus, and then Atlantic City, then the combined continents of the Americas. She had massive pyramids built in all the corners so that they could be connected to spell out her name.

And she was just getting started.

By her twenty-fifth birthday, she'd become the wealthiest earth-born person in the galaxy and made the Forbes-Orion Infinite Growth list three years running. She was profiled in *Timeless* magazine. She amassed a collection of art and kept in in her Paris estate. The Paris estate was so well envied through the rest of the galaxy, other places were merely known as the Paris of This or That – The Paris of the Orient, The Paris of Triton, The Paris of Orion, The Paris of the Platinum Star Cluster.

She married twice before reaching her thirties; both husbands were assassinated, as was the custom, by jealous lovers.

The earth was hers, and hers alone, when the King's Regent made a gift of it to her to celebrate her fortieth birthday.

She loved birthdays, and insisted every carnival be a celebration of someone's birthday. She would find someone on some random outer mining colony through a simple database search and send the Traveling Carnival to that part of the galaxy. She showered gifts on the lucky recipients, often enough to buy them out of the mining life; in turn, the Emissaries of those colonies gave her all manner of priceless gifts. She stored them all, often unseen, in Greater Britain and the Australian archipelago, as they were so rarely used.

By her fiftieth birthday, she'd been made honorary queen over eleven outposts and star systems, and no fewer than twenty halls of fame had immortalized her in statues of bronze, marble, stardust, and crepe paper. A semi-persistent wormhole bore her name, as did a hundred billion children of no less than a thousand varying races. Every clown in the galaxy was suspected of being on her payroll. She'd seen the dusty diamond migration, the cascades of the Auroras, and Elvis in concert – the kind of things most people only dreamt of. She had more money than God – which, to the best of anyone's recollection, was a feat no one had ever accomplished before, and – since God controlled the banks – maybe no one ever would again. She had a dozen dozen harems, a beautiful fountain pen, seventeen heirs, and the last bottle of champagne. So when she disappeared, everyone understood why.

She'd come back to our time, with the ever-young hotshot dark star pilot as her only companion, and now resides in a small flat in Brooklyn.

John Urbancik

16 JANUARY

It had been a fine spring day. The sky was blue, the sun extraordinarily pleasant, the country fair in full swing. They devoured pies in one tent, placed blue ribbons on bovines in another, and had all the thrill rides running at full tilt. You couldn't get away from the noise of it all.

If you'd expected something to happen, it would've been in the Haunted Maze or the Hall of Mirrors. You might've feared the roller coaster hopping the tracks or someone getting sick on The Rotor. Maybe a bull would escape and gore townsfolk on the midway or a clown would suddenly succumb to latent homicidal tendencies.

It was none of those things.

In the Kiddie Korner, with its Tea Cups and carousel, there was an innocuous looking ride called The Balloon Race. A half dozen seats with balloons – I don't mean the kind you blow up or use to drift lazily over rolling fields – these balloons were the size of a man, very likely hollow, probably light, and certainly made of plastic if not some sort of aluminum frame. You could send your four year old up for a race. You were never quite sure who won, and neither were they.

The gondolas rose perhaps eight feet into the sky at the end of long mechanical arms. They swayed very slightly.

That was it. That was the whole ride.

Some teenagers decided they wanted to race. They let a few of the little ones go ahead of them so they could each sit one each to a gondola and have them all. Boys, girls – a lot of acne and hair care products and all the latest expensive fashions of the junior high set. Six of them. Laughing. Possibly drinking beer or getting high just a few moments earlier.

The bell sounded and the self-proclaimed balloons started to lift. Red, orange, yellow, green, blue, and purple rocked gently and swayed. The teenagers yelled jabs at each other. Clearly, they believed there would be a winner.

That beautifully perfect spring day, there was no winner.

The green balloon broke first. You could hear the metal snap over all the din of the fair. Then it tore away with a crunching sound.

Orange followed.

Then blue and yellow both. By this time, all the crowds throughout the fair had gone quiet; the pigs had stopped squealing and the auctioneer ceased calling for bids.

Teenagers always believed they'd live forever. Maybe sometimes, they did.

The running rides in the rest of the fair had to finish their runs. The games that didn't play their own music fell preternaturally silent. The mechanical steeplechase ceased running.

The purple gondola and balloon was the last to rip free. The red, having reached the highest height of the ride, stayed there.

The other five floated away.

No, they were not filled with helium. Nor were they filled with rocket fuel. Yet they rocketed up from the fair, like actual balloons. The race, at least for us bystanders, ended when the balloons were swallowed by clouds. We never saw the teenagers or the aluminum and/or plastic balloons again.

Only the red remained, a boy who, to this date, has never uttered another word. He must wonder, even still, what had made him so special that he was spared.

But sometimes, I suspect, he must ask – at least in his dreams – why he'd been excluded.

17 JANUARY

Picture the girl: an acrobat, a contortionist, short black hair glistening in the spotlight like every bead of sweat on every muscle. Untouchable, there on the stage. Unattainable. Like a goddess on display.

Six, seven performances later, you know her routine; but you also know she's something other than human. Her eyes aren't a natural shade of blue at all, and surely they glow, ever so slightly, when the lights go down.

Has she seen you? Has she made and maintained eye contact? It's not possible, improbable, unlikely, and absurd. It's a dream, albeit not the most original.

The way she moves: so slowly, with deliberate and precise intention. The way she bends and twists, you assume she's missing bones and those that remain aren't made of bone at all but soft, pliable rubber.

It's not until the eleventh show that you realize she's an android. There's so much noise, it practically drowns out the mechanized whirs and the clicking of gears. That explains everything. Even the sweat is artificial, every bead at every show forming in the exact same spots.

She's a machine, and you begin to wonder about the programs that run her, the lines of code and algorithms in her head. That time she made eye contact, she must've filed the image of your face in her database.

What kind of coolant pumps through her veins to prevent meltdown during her act?

She probably doesn't have vocal abilities. You've never heard her speak. It would be extraneous. More than her inventor needed, and therefore not a good reason to delay implementation.

But her inventor? Who? Does that person work through the night on advancing the device? Giving her speech and maybe thought processes? Is she meant to become some form of artificial intelligence, or is she merely an automaton incapable of varying her cycles?

There's a tinkerer behind the scenes, a man or woman who built and maintains the machine in an underlit toolshed filled with old fashioned clockwork tools and assorted cables, tubes, oils, and lubricants.

Maybe fifteen performances later, you've decided you must meet her maker. You've ascertained that a series of only three guards work this tent, disguised as carnies, though there may be more behind the stage. A team of low wage college kids clean up between the aisles after every show. You wait until the final show of the night, when it's darkest and the kids are tired and anxious to get to the bar.

You use the shadows to your advantage. Though you've got a cover story ready to deploy, it's not required. You evade detection. The guards, after the last show, seem to have gone.

You sneak behind the scenes.

Backstage is a maze of curtains and sandbags and scenery props. There's a trunk for the juggler; you almost trip over it. There's not much light back here.

You follow a route based primarily on what you've been able to hear, from outside the tent, over the past few weeks. Finally, you find the contortionist's dressing room.

She sits, perfectly still, on a stool, her bare back facing you. Where are the tools and gadgets? What's with the spare leotards and – is that a pair of jeans folded neatly on the table?

Where is her maker?

You clear your throat to attract the attention of someone you can't see. The android's head turns slightly to one side. You hear the mechanism of it. She doesn't turn far enough to see you, and she doesn't say a word.

"You," you tell her, approaching with genuine admiration, "are a thing of beauty. Absolutely remarkable. I almost believed in the illusion entirely."

"Almost?" the android's maker – a woman still hidden in shadows – asks.

"The noise of the carnival hides the tell-tale sounds," you say, "and of course the exterior is seamless."

"Maybe not entirely."

"But unseen," you say. "My own machines aren't nearly so perfect."

The maker steps out from the shadows. She holds a frightening bit of metal in her hand. It's a gun. It didn't immediately register as a gun because you expected batteries or memory cards or almost anything else.

"So you," she says, this older woman who looks very much like the android. "You've discovered my secret. Now I must kill you."

At point blank range, she shoots you in the chest.

The noise is deafening. It scrambles the microphone, creates an alarming amount of feedback. You try to look down at the bullet hole, but it seems to have damaged a servo; the head will not tilt, no matter how you jiggle the joystick.

"That," you say into the microphone, "was not very nice."

The maker examines your avatar, peering closely into the eyes, at the pores, at the ears and the strands of hair. Finally, she steps back, nods once, and says, "Quite an achievement yourself. I'm impressed."

You smile. Your avatar does not. You say, "Thank you. Perhaps we can meet in the flesh. Without the gun."

She does smile. "I'd like that."

18 JANUARY

He built his first carnival with a knock-off version of Play-Doh. It consisted of a Ferris wheel, a carousel, and an oversized ringmaster. It was rather short-lived. And, let's be honest: it was an abstraction, the suggestion of shapes rather than an accurate representation. But he was only four.

Later, he built a Ferris wheel in spun sugar, a carousel with matchsticks, and a roller coaster that would best be described as a mixed-media construction. That was the first to actually work – if you set the miniature cars at the pinnacle of the first climb and gave them a push.

He also painted. And he dabbled in photography, albeit primarily to provide his paintings with the right angles and the proper play of light and shadow. You couldn't rely on someone else to accidentally see what you saw.

At nineteen, he got permission from the city council to renovate the carnival in the park. It was old, not well-cared for, and mostly sat there behind yellow caution tape awaiting its inevitable dismantling. The council gave him only a small stipend to pay for supplies; the rest he got from soliciting donations from the public and selling photographic prints of the dilapidated and neglected horses. The project took most of three years and the assistance of seventeen volunteers – some for a few weekends, many for a few months at a time.

Though he was not paid for the project, it earned him the cover of two different magazines and his first gallery show. Some of his paintings did not sell; the ones that did were all priced at four digits.

He built a working scale-model carnival after that, complete with lights, a Ferris wheel that spun, and a calliope sound emerging from the carousel. There were another six rides, a midway filled with games and foods – not edible. He was convinced to auction it off; the carnival fetched six digits and gained him another cover, this one on a national magazine of some prestige.

After that, a Mysterious Benefactor sent a woman to offer the artist this proposal: design and oversee the construction of a full-sized amusement park. It should contain at least two roller coasters – one for kids and one immense – several stages, and anything the artist thought it should require. Two sums of money were mentioned: a starting budget and a salary. He would be made part owner and reap profits from the venture for the rest of his life.

How could he refuse?

He needed time to study, and to work with professional craftsmen; the land had already been laid aside, but ground-breaking occurred later than planned. After that, despite the typical delays and cost overruns, construction progressed at a wonderful pace.

The artist's amusement park grew and expanded. A second location opened twelve years later. The Mysterious Benefactor – a descendant of circus money – remained anonymous, though of course the artist eventually met the source of his funds.

He also eventually married the woman who'd been sent to make the original proposal.

A third location is set to open next May, this one with four intertwining roller coasters. The artist still walks through his parks with his camera and later paints what he shoots. And last summer, on the shores of Daytona Beach, he'd constructed a carnival in sand. Just for fun.

19 JANUARY

The couple approaches the Fortune Teller machine at the back corner of the tent. A gypsy woman's face – which may, in fact, be a real gypsy woman's face preserved by gypsy magic or formaldehyde – sits at the top of an obvious plastic facsimile of a body. The glass case includes a variety of tarot cards and tea cups, a scrying glass, ribbons and beads, and a small card giving some history of the great Madame Fortuna, whose real name – the card reveals – is Gabrielle. The card makes no mention of her daughter.

The couple feeds the machine the necessary coins. A pre-recorded voice warns that the future is sometimes unclear and suggests they wait just a moment longer for theirs to be prepared. The machine seems to need more time than is usual to spit out the stiff little card.

The couple goes away pleased.

But what really happened?

Inside the machine, as the couple approaches, an alarm is sounded by the lookout. "Incoming!" he calls, watching through a peephole in the plastic body of the gypsy woman. "A couple, male and female, young, holding hands!"

One of the seers, inevitably, says, "Just as expected."

A board is checked, on which they've scribbled the name of today's foreseen visitors along with estimated times. This grid reveals a particular oracle, who had bet on their arrival and therefore wins a cash prize. "Jill," someone says. "Jack. Just on time."

Often, the fortunes are prepared ahead of time; but on occasion, as today, they need to see the fortune seeker to get a clear reading of what's ahead. Cards are consulted, crystals gazed into, leaves interpreted, mirrors viewed, and a team of oracles, seers, and prophets – under the direction of a veteran foreman – observes all the threads, the interactions and calamities, the truths and falsehoods, and – well, everything.

This information is gathered and delivered to the poets, who condense it all into something simple yet vague – and accurate. Their words are given to the artists who, with grand sweeping strokes of oversized brushes dipped in ink, write out the fortunes on a card.

In this case, the fortune reads: "Your future together is long and happy, and what trials you face will make you stronger."

They write the words even as the plastic gypsy hands move in such a way as to mimic something mystical.

This is not the way of all Fortune Teller machines at all carnivals. Some are refilled with new cards from a warehouse outside of Myrtle Beach.

20 JANUARY

There's a strange kind of logic which insists everything must be true. Infinite worlds and parallel dimensions and alternative universes collide with various misinterpretations of quantum theory to transform all possibilities into truth, however improbable.

This, Jack concluded, after a certain amount of whiskey, lent him a profound depth of knowledge nobody shared – which, he also realized, was just as untrue as it was true, as the realms of possibility were broad and without limit.

He started with his bar tab. It seemed simple enough: he suspected some mystery woman had taken care of it entirely.

The bartender, although he seemed momentarily confused, said, "Yes, that's exactly what happened." Then he pointed out the woman, a blonde bombshell from the 50's, a sort of femme fatale in a black dress. And while Jack appreciated the choice of attire, he wondered why she couldn't be a redhead.

Of course, it had been a trick of the light. Her hair, as he approached, fell about her face like molten lava.

"Hello," she said.

"Hello."

He liked a little bit of mystery. Maybe he'd never learn her name at all. In his mind, he decided to call her Red. It seemed appropriate.

"Are we done with this place yet?" she asked.

They left together. Her little Italian sports car waited outside, even if no one had noticed it before.

"Oh, this is too easy," Jack said, only partly a complaint.

"What do you mean?"

"Where are you from?"

"Here and there," she said. "Paris. New York. I lived in Tokyo for a while, too. My father was a businessman until I forced him into an early retirement."

"And how is it you're interested in someone like me?" he asked. It was a genuine question. He knew there had to be an answer – all things were possible – and he wanted to know it.

"I like the way you look at things," she said.

She knew. She might not have known the way he knew, but she had the gist of it. The essence. Enough to understand his sudden power.

She added, "I like a man in control."

"Shouldn't there be a challenge?" he asked.

"You mean a quest?" Red smiled, and it was enough to hurt his heart. He hadn't meant that at all, but he couldn't argue that it had been a distinct possibility. "Of course there's a quest. I want to hear a song."

"Any particular song?" Jack asked.

"Not a song you'll ever hear on the radio," Red said. "Not a song you've ever heard before. You won't find it on the internet. It was recorded in '67, I think, and it's what you'd call Avant-garde."

He had no idea what she was talking about. But it was possible he had known; after all, he'd listened to The Beatles, and didn't everybody know about their never-released 14 minute "Carnival of Light"?

"I know the song you mean," Jack said. "But there's only one copy in existence, the master tape, and that's in Paul McCartney's vault somewhere."

"Sir Paul McCartney," she reminded him.

"Right."

"Doesn't he have a house near here?"

Here, Jack knew, was the middle of nowhere, and nobody who was anybody had a house near here. Yet it was entirely possible someone like Sir Paul McCartney would have just such a place to house so special a vault as the one that held the rarest audio track known to exist.

"Of course he does," Jack finally said.

Red tossed him the keys to her car. "Let's go."

He eased behind the wheel and nearly cried. In another, parallel world, he must've cried – all things, remember – but here he held himself in check. She sat beside him like a Bond girl played by a redheaded Brigitte Bardot. The engine screamed, the machine responded to his every thought, and they left the bar quickly behind.

The road, since it was entirely possible, was his alone, without taxis or police cruisers or Datsuns. There was a brief moment when he had to outrace a German sports car filled with men – not from Germany – with machine guns. As unlikely as it seemed, the chase raised his heart up to an astounding pace.

He pulled up to the circle in front of Sir Paul McCartney's mansion, which must always have been right here. Red put a hand briefly on his thigh, high and inside. It was like being touched by a star. She said, "I'm so excited."

They walked up the drive. The former Beatle, himself, met them at the door, because it was entirely feasible he'd been expecting them. "Come on in," he said. "Everything's ready."

Everything included a massive vegetarian buffet, a variety of whiskeys because a perfect host always knew his guest's favorite drink, and an old-fashioned reel ready to play.

"This is, you understand, the master copy," Sir Paul McCartney said.

"I feel like I've been waiting to hear it all my life," Red admitted.

Sir Paul McCartney then said to Jack: "If you would do the honors."

Jack pressed play.

"Carnival of Light" burst from the speakers. It was a cacophony Jack couldn't understand. It hurt his eyes. He could barely see through the tears.

Perhaps he had stretched the boundaries of possibility too far?

He rubbed his eyes, found himself returned to the bar. He ordered another whiskey. He kept his eyes open for Red.

21 JANUARY

Not all carnivals are inbred with a kind of magic. This story, however, is not about one of those mundane carnivals. The carnies in this story are all descended from one of the great Romani lines. The fortunes they offer are more accurate, the colors in their balloons more vibrant, the horses in their carousel more lively.

On a cool night in early winter, after the traditional traveling season, when those mundane outfits have already set up camp in Florida, the magic carnivals gather in an undisclosed location – never the same from year to year – and throw themselves a fete.

This is not a night for thrill rides or games of chance; nor is it a night for cheap calliope music pumped through undersized speakers. This is a night for the musicians. Violins. Trumpets. Pianos instead of harpsichords.

And this is a night for masks. All things are secret when the carnival travelling tribes gather. All things are permitted. Love. Murder. Spell casting. Dance.

A huge bonfire will light the night sky, and they will dance from dusk till break of day. At that time, lovers will disentangle, poisons will be discarded, and masks will be shed.

Purely by accident, on a cool winter morning, I discovered the remains of just such an event. There were a thousand and one masks of porcelain and lace and papier-mâché and ribbons. I collected them all. The fire pit still smoldered. A broken violin had been left behind. Also a few bodies.

It took me a long time. I'm not adept at magic, and also I had to learn a new skillset, but I repaired and restored that violin. I was convinced anyone could play a magic-infused carnival instrument, but no bow I tried would bring forth any beautiful notes.

Although I tried several bows, I hesitated to allow anyone else to touch the violin. I feared some of its magic would be lost to the violinist and there would be less for me. The very idea made me sad, and I felt quite certain there should be no sadness associated with this kind of wonder.

Eventually, I realized my error.

So I waited until that cool winter night returned, as it did once every year, and I donned one of the masks I had recovered. Then I walked to the beach with the violin under my chin, confident the mundane bow would not be a hindrance.

I had never heard such a magnificent note as the one I played then. I played a song in its entirety – or the song played me, I never could rightly say. When I finished, I saw I had an audience: a carnival girl in her butterfly mask, more beautiful even than the song. And though I saw no bonfire and heard no band, though no one danced around us drinking mystic drinks, I knew I had discovered – or been discovered – by an honest, bone-deep love.

One night every winter I see my lover. This is why I wait so anxiously for the carnival season to end.

22 JANUARY

On a Friday night in May, Zeus took the kids – some of the kids, as it's hard to keep track of them all – to the fair. It went about as well as you'd think.

Heracles spent dollar after dollar failing to ring the bell at the top of the high striker until he finally busted the hammer in frustration.

Aphrodite spent the entire night at the kissing booth and made a lot of money.

The twins – Artemis and Apollo – went round and round on the carousel until they realized neither could win the race; then they brought the horses to life and raced out of the carnival, causing several wrecks and at least one fire.

Athena took over for the guess your weight guy. She guessed weights and ages and hometowns and favorite colors – and when she finally got one guy's color wrong, around midnight, she showed him the head of Medusa. He was petrified.

Perseus won every game of skill and chance, collecting a large supply of prizes which he then gave away.

At one of the food courts, Persephone tasted a half dozen deep fried concoctions, the repercussions of which we'll be feeling for a very long time.

Hephaestus spent his time in the stables examining the horses and their shoes, complaining bitterly of shoddy workmanship.

The Fates had a long discussion with the tarot card reader, revealing her fortune in minute detail, leaving the pool girl utterly devastated and unable ever to speak again.

Nemesis got into a fight with one of the carnies.

And Ares re-organized the bumper cards.

Zeus never noticed any of this, having transformed himself into a corn dog to seduce a sword swallower named Helen.

23 JANUARY

There's a girl with blue tinted black hair. She'll tell you she's Roma, though of course it's a lie. She'll probably tell you a truth every once in a while to convince you; and you will be convinced, as her powers are true and beyond reproach.

Her face is pale but brightly made up, with red around her eyes in long, dipping curves, and blue on her lips to match the hair. Every eyelash is in place. The diamond on her nose sparkles – even in moonlight.

She wears a huge red flower, an explosion of a flower, in her hair, and she'll tell you an anxious suitor gave it to her just an hour ago.

And when she looks at you, her eyes so deep and perfect, a bronze flicked with emerald, you almost feel like she's tearing at the heart of your soul to uncover your deepest desires.

When she speaks, her accent is vague and indeterminate, as though she picked up some Catalan and Ukrainian and Brazilian and Dutch and Slavic in her travels. She'll tell you she's travelled to a great many places, but she'll only name St. Louis and Boston – and sometimes Tucson.

She throws winks as though it's her greatest power, and I've seen them steal the breath from grizzled men and make Catholic school girls blush.

Ah – but what's her name? She'll tell you Jezebel or Cleopatra or Sue, depending on her mood; and she's probably never used the same name twice. She uses syllables as a form of flirtation and rolls her name off her tongue like whiskey and spice.

She travels with me, with the carnival, so you can be assured she has been to many places, including those she forgot to mention. There's magic in her, in her every movement, in the way she angles her hip and the way she wrinkles her eye. She could do anything she wants here: con you into tossing rings, reveal your romantic fortunes, twirl through the air into the waiting hands of the acrobat. She can juggle oranges. I've seen her do it – idly, as if just to pass the time. She might have transformed a magician's act into something brilliant, wonderful, and magical.

She bakes.

She's older than she looks and older than you'd guess but she'll never reveal an age – not even a false one. You'll never meet her mother; and if you're favored by fortune, you'll never meet her sister. She'll tell you she has a brother or three, but I think there are five, and they all work the carnival circuit.

She makes promises. All sorts of promises. Illicit promises, secret promises, dark promises, innocent promises. She'll raise your hopes and your fears. I've never seen her keep a promise except that once; it had not been made to someone like you or someone like me.

But you know she loves you, or she likes you, or at least she isn't offended by the breath you steal from the earth, because you've been back every night this week for a churro or a biscuit or caramel apple or elephant ears, and though you're sure she's done it to others, she hasn't mixed poison into your spices yet.

24 JANUARY

"It's like a carnival in my mouth."

What she meant: that particular combination of flavors was vibrant and rich, not merely delicious but extraordinarily so.

He should've asked her to be his wife. They could've run away together on a long honeymoon to some Caribbean island, got drunk off of rum and each other, maybe learned to play the steel drums or get her hair braided or ride jet skis on the Atlantic.

Instead, he decided to devote his life to food: the creation of meals, the serving to diners of their own personal mouthfuls of carnival. What he lacked in culinary training and business acumen, he made up for with unbridled enthusiasm and confidence, and money.

He secured a location, hired an artisan skilled in his craft to design a sign to hang outside, gathered a wait staff and a hostess, and employed one of the region's most talented graphic designers to perfect a menu format.

Opening night – a soft opening for friends and former colleagues and a couple of lucky radio station winners – went well enough, in that everyone got food and left full, and the wait staff made a fair amount of tips.

But the true opening followed a week later, when he served the general public and food critics and the ex-girlfriend who had said, that not-so-long-ago night, "It's like a carnival in my mouth."

What she'd meant was: kiss me, kiss me now and forever, kiss me with confidence and tenderness and passion and reckless abandon and love.

He called the restaurant *Carnivale*. It was meant to be a fine dining experience, so he'd been tasteful when hanging masks and assorted artwork on the walls. He'd hired a pianist and a wandering violinist to softly serenade the diners. They worked both individually and together, under what most considered to be a perfection of lighting.

The most notable review stated: "The food is, as described, a carnival in your mouth – if you mean it tastes of sawdust and cowboy sweat, with a nuanced aroma of livestock and manure. I would've been more pleased if I'd been served a plate of funnel cakes with canned strawberries and a side of cotton candy. But I'm not being entirely fair; the food consisted, not of canned or magic ingredients, but the freshest and finest produce and cuts of meat. The chef, however, combined these wonderful ingredients in the most discordant of ways, as though they'd never seen a spice – as though they meant to approximate the taste of a century-old carousel calliope: rusty, shallow, and out of tune."

He called his ex the next morning. She admitted she still loved him. All was not lost. The dinner he'd made her had been good enough, but it wasn't what she'd really wanted.

That day, he hired a chef, an honest chef with talent, skills, experience, and a high level of taste; then he asked his ex to reconsider their current lack of an arrangement.

25 JANUARY

It's a flea market. People put price tags on useless junk and try to pass it off as treasures. You can find genuine belt buckles, Matchbox cars, mason jars filled with all sorts of pickled stuff, and – sometimes, if you're lucky and know what you're looking for – an honest treasure.

Jill sought nothing but treasure.

She didn't need kitchy salt and pepper shakers. Nor did she need a 19th century stew pot. She didn't need questionable additions for her vinyl collection. She didn't need an unopened bottle of Coca-Cola from the 70's – or any other decade.

She did drink some lemonade, but only because she was thirsty and they were using real lemons and real sugar to make it.

One woman tried to convince her to buy a baby name book. One man wanted to give her a slim pamphlet of Bible verses. Another talked about snakes. A younger man tried to sell her a variety of American and Canadian coins older than he was; then he tried to ask her for a date.

Jill wandered through collections of unwanted clothing, sun-faded comic books, an assortment of baseballs retrieved at Yankee Stadium.

An elderly gentleman sitting in a stall full of harmonicas said, "You're in the wrong place."

"Excuse me?"

He looked up at her as though he'd never looked up at anyone ever before. He said, "This is a bazaar." When she didn't immediately respond, he added, "You're looking for the fair."

"The fair?"

"The midway."

She smiled. She said, "Thank you. I'll think about it." But she had no intention to go to the fair, or even to look for it, as she had not even known it was in town.

"Wait." The old man pushed himself to his feet, which appeared to require a bit of effort, and grabbed a particular harmonica – just like any of the rest – from his stall. "You won't go. Stubborn girl. Least you can do is take this."

He thrust that one harmonica at her. He said, "I don't want your money. This is important."

She glanced at the instrument briefly, then said, "Thank you." She slipped it into her bag as the old man deposited himself in his chair. He mumbled under his breath and watched her from under his brow.

She left. She left the stall and, shortly thereafter, the flea market.

Jill didn't remember the harmonica until after dinner, when she searched in her purse for something else. She had no history with harmonicas and knew of no songs that needed one. Cowboys played them around campfires, right?

She attempted to blow through it. The sound was not a note, but a mess, jumbled and haphazard and without architecture.

Under other circumstances, on another evening with another harmonica, she probably would've put it down somewhere and forgotten it.

But her jumble of sounds had been answered by a riotous noise and a flood of light bursting in through every window.

Then her front door opened.

A car rolled in on a track. It was like something you'd see in an amusement park, with two rows of seats and bearing passengers and safety bars.

The tracks, she realized, wound through her living room to the kitchen, then upstairs. As the first car started its climb, the kids inside pointing excitedly at the pictures on her wall, another car entered.

"What's going on?" she asked, though she knew full well no one here would provide a satisfactory answer. No one did. She ran outside, just before another car burst in her front door. A line of people waited to go in. A teenaged girl with a tattoo on her face – no, with an incredible bout of acne – collected tickets.

Jill went to the girl. "What's..."

The girl smiled at her. "Wait your turn."

"But it's my house," Jill said.

The girl looked at her as though Jill was the wrong flavor of ice cream. She said, "It's everybody's house."

Jill looked at her house again. It wasn't everybody's house. It was hers. The girl turned away sharply to load up the next passengers.

Right. Jill knew how a thing like this happened. Magic. And she knew how it could be undone: the same magic. She blew a mouthful of air through the harmonica.

Nothing changed.

The old man, ambling along with the rest of the line, said, "I'm glad you made it."

"What have you done?" Jill asked.

The old man scowled. "Stupid girl, I didn't do anything. You're the one who desperately needs fun in your life. So here it is. You did this. Yours is, for at least tonight, the fun house. Now join me inside."

26 JANUARY

I died.

I'm not going to get into the gruesome details. Let's just leave it as my sudden death was unexpected and, if you ask me, unwarranted.

But this isn't about what I deserved or what I earned. I lived my life the way I did, and for that I will be both punished and rewarded. Of this, I have no doubt.

Death took me. Like I said, it was a jolt. One moment, I'm alive and well – or as well as circumstances permitted – the next, I'm standing just outside the ticket gate at an oversized carnival.

The sounds alone were enough to knock you over: all manner of bells and buzzers and music, all the barkers competing for their marks, laughter and screams and the clickity clacks of rides that might've been new a century ago.

I knew already that I was dead. There was no mistaking what had just happened. The sky here was twilight, a deep swirl of reds and oranges and dark clouds, as if I needed some sort of metaphor.

And I wasn't alone. The carnival was doing a hell of a business. People lined up for every ride I could see. They pushed through each other to get at the candied apples and turkey legs. That was inside; out here, a small queue had formed in front of the ticket booth and a bunch of people, alone and in small groups, milled about, perhaps hesitant to enter what the sign proclaimed to be The Carnival of Death.

I joined the line. When I died, I had money in my pockets, but here I wore jeans I'm not sure I'd worn before and my pockets were empty. I didn't realize this until it was my turn at the front of the line.

"That's okay, hon," the woman said to me, handing me five tickets. "Everyone gets a chance. Go on it. Enjoy yourself. See what you might find."

As it turned out, everything cost one ticket. You want to ride the double roller coaster that seemed to stretch all the way from here to Jersey? One ticket. Interested in having your face painted like a clown or a butterfly? One ticket. Hungry for churros? One ticket. Try your luck at the basketball hoop? You get the picture.

I wandered a bit, trying to take it all in, but you simply couldn't. This wasn't Coney Island or Great Adventure or Disney World. This was a bright, colorful, vibrant nation, maybe a whole planet, and it grew as you walked through it.

I spent my first ticket at a kissing booth. It was worth it.

I spent my second ticket on cinnamon almonds, which were delicious.

I spent my third ticket to see a light and water show with sentient smoke and brilliant colors and a girl dressed up as a mermaid. I know it sounds strange, but the show was great, and I left the hall singing its theme song in my head.

Obviously, I had no plan, and I had given no thought to what would happen when I used my last ticket. Maybe I'd get more. Or maybe my time in this waystation would be over and I'd move on to whatever was next. But as I gripped my last two tickets, I felt a sudden uncertainty. I wasn't afraid, I wouldn't say that. I was enjoying myself and I didn't want it to end.

So I held onto those two tickets with a miser's grip and continued wandering. I passed a tent promising dancing hippos and a machine that foretold futures. Seemed a little late, if you ask me. I lingered at a game of skill, something to do with tossing softballs at milk jugs; but I stopped at one of the games of chance.

Among the prize at the Wheel of Fortune – the thing that caught my eye – was a packet of fifty more tickets. There were dozens of possibilities, including a hearty congratulations, a certificate of authenticity, a pink bow tie, and a glass of hot chocolate.

Admittedly, I'd just died, so I wasn't feeling that I was on a roll of good luck and everything would fall my way. On the other hand, I had just died – wouldn't an extended stay at the carnival be some sort of karmic balance?

I gave the girl my ticket. She spun the wheel. It stood upright, and the tongue slapped between each peg with a thunderous snap that, at least to me, drowned out all the other carnival noises.

Too late, I realized other prizes – if they could be called that – included a two week stay in the palace dungeon, something with knives I hesitate to describe, and a poisoned apple.

As the wheel slowed, I saw horrible options pass by along with emerald rings, slow dances, and giant stuffed panda bears.

But I didn't win any of that. The wheel stopped on Rejuvenation.

That's when I woke up here. You might not believe me. That's your choice. I don't care. But I still have one unused ticket as proof.

27 JANUARY

Ten thousand years from today, in a bar on the south side of some space port city – a grimy, moon-shadowed town with as much heartache as hope – two of the old gods will meet, by chance, after an extended time apart, and they will discuss today.

The world will change twice within the lifetime of some our youngest citizens, and another hundred times or more before this chance encounter. The old gods, eternal though they may be, will become more and more useless. The forests they once occupied will be completely and utterly gone, even if replaced by new forests. People will not share the same drinks, even if they call them by the same names. Their whiskey will be, by our standards – and by the standards of gods – unrecognizable. Humanity will have replaced itself with newer versions, more than once, upgrading as desired or required, adapting, adopting, re-creating in its own distorted vision.

The old gods will also change. It's the nature of old gods to blend into the times. It's how they become old gods. Young gods are often reckless and ridiculous; they don't always become old gods. They don't always establish a name for themselves. They can't always foster belief or idolatry or religion.

Not all gods become myths.

The two gods will raise a glass of what they'll eventually call whiskey and drink a toast in memory of those old forests, those lost civilizations, those half-remembered humans they knew so briefly.

The two gods will shed a tear or two, but they will also laugh, and as is often the case when gods gather, they will sing, and they will dance, and they will create magic. Men and women – and the other varieties soon to be available – will join those two gods for this one night, and it will last for weeks.

Such is the way of gods, young or old. They will bestow gifts and great boons and take mates and break hearts both metaphorical and physical. They will make a name for themselves, even if only briefly, and they will accept that they may have no one else left but each other.

They will be reminded of all this because of a Ferris wheel in a questionable spaceport city ten thousand years hence.

Because tonight, this year, in the middle of a country fair in the flat center of this country, these gods – as yet young gods, I'm sorry to say – will meet under the Ferris wheel and draw their weapons – lightning, wind, hail, brimstone, coyotes, fire ants, vultures – and they will not relent. These two young gods, tonight, in the flashing lights and with a blinding soundtrack, will create names for themselves.

28 JANUARY

I am power.

I am electricity.

I am your pulse, your breath, the song on your tongue, the rhythm in your stride.

There are, in this world, a great many mysteries. Many are natural. Some are misunderstandings. Quite a few are completely artificial and, oftentimes, unnecessary. I am a different kind of mystery, the kind without apparent cause, the kind without solution.

You walk with your feet, you see with your eyes, you feel with your hands or your heart; but I am the reason you know things. I am the reason you question. I am the cause of your seeking, the spark that ignites you, the thrill that inspires you.

I am the space between spaces, the void between the nucleus and the proton. I am cosmic dust and the galactic eye and the thread that binds you to everything you've ever seen or known.

Maybe it would help you more if I described what I am not. I am not eternal. I am not divine. I am neither the god you worship nor the god you don't.

I am not you.

I am not me, either.

I'm not easy to explain.

I'm not the wind or the magnetic poles, I'm not the rings around the planets, I'm not the stars or the snowflakes or the grains of sand in the desert.

I'm not something you're capable of grasping – not yet.

Maybe it would help more if I explain our relationship. You and I. I am not your father or your mother, not your sibling, not a distant cousin who calls begging money. I'm not your landlord or your tenant. I'm not your totem, your guide, your guardian angel.

We are not kin, not in any way that makes sense, though of course we are each made up of the same stuff that existed at the start of this universe and will cease to exist when this universe is finally extinguished.

I am not your doppelganger or evil twin or parallel you. I'm not your servant, even if I may, at times, seem to serve. Nor am I your master. I ask nothing of you.

This isn't working out very well.

Okay; what are you to me? You are my sunrise and my moonrise and my trumpets and my pleasant aroma. You are my diamond and my coal dust. You are my benefactor and my heir and my friend and my lover, albeit not in any way you'd accept.

You are my ride through this journey, my roller coaster, my lightning loop. You are my joy – my carnival, my play.

You know what? Forget all this. It doesn't matter. We need no reasons. It's enough to simply breathe. So: thank you.

29 JANUARY

It's a tough life, being a clown.

First, you've got to go to clown college, learn all about the great clowns who came before you – Joseph Grimwalde, Emmett Kelly, Lou Jacobs – and you've got to learn how to drive a small car with seventy of your kin stacked in with you.

You have to decide if you want to join the circus in an age very unlike the heyday of the Ringling Brothers, spend your life doing children's birthday parties – which might seem like fun until you're twisting your thousandth balloon poodle – or maybe the rodeo, which comes with its own inherent dangers.

How much call is there in this internet age for harlequins and tramps?

Will you be a happy clown or a sad clown? Because, while it is painted on your face, your image will stay with you forever, and you run the risk of taking on your face as your temperament.

You'll have to join an association. It's not just doctors and lawyers and screenwriters who've got guilds. You might attend conventions and find yourself surrounded by other clowns, both failed and successful, as well as jugglers and magicians – and this would be a regular thing for you.

You'll face the derision of teenagers.

Your best friends will probably also be clowns. Think of the implications of that.

There's just not a lot of respect for clowns today. Except maybe from the coulrophobes, who will break into a cold sweat at the merest indication of greasepaint, who cower at the slightest sound of pantomime.

The truth is, it's not easy work. It's physically demanding. The hours are grueling. You're on the road as often as rock stars without the advantages of groupies.

Clowns have to be multi-talented. They're part mime, character actor, balloonist, juggler, gymnast, contortionist, jester, wise man, tightrope walker, horse whisperer, ringmaster, musician, acrobat, fighter, lover, showman, bicyclist, and owner of a menagerie of rubber chickens.

And for all that, you'll still be considered the fool.

Maybe it's intentional. Maybe a form of misdirection to lull the rest of us, the non-clowns in the world, into believing there can be joy and laughter and, most importantly, mirth, as some sort of secret plan to take over the world.

Maybe we'd be better off if the clowns took over. But then I look at the state of our elected officials, our government and politicians, and I realize the true clowns have always been in control. You see? That's exactly the kind of reason clowns get no respect.

30 JANUARY

Free day.
Go listen to some new music.

31 JANUARY

The Last Carnival rolled out of town in the hour before dawn. A caravan of trucks, vans, station wagons, and motorcycles left a trail of dust behind them, and nothing else but memories and cheap stuffed prizes and more than a few broken hearts.

Maybe they took a few children with them – runaways to join the travelling life of acrobats and illusion.

By the time the sun hit the town again, they were long gone – west, away from the scorching light of day. Colors bled away in the stark, harsh reality. Shadows stood crisp and menacing. Somewhere, a child kicked a tin can in the street. Bars opened up early. The only question on anyone's mind: would there be enough whiskey?

The heat came quickly and without mercy. Everything in town slowed down to accommodate it. Even heartbeats. Even breathing.

Someone – somebody mean and nasty, the kind who relishes the suffering of others – tore down all the posters, removing all evidence the Last Carnival had ever pitched a tent anywhere near these parts.

Jill knew she would die with the town, but she rejected this fate. She made an assumption: the road west would lead, not just out of town, not to some mythical pasture of green, but straight to the carnival.

She didn't have to say anything. She packed a bag with a change of clothes, a bit of food and some precious water, and climbed onto her bike. When she pulled back on the throttle, letting the engine roar its intent, it was not a way of saying goodbye. It was, instead, an introduction to a new life, a new Jill, a new horizon, and with a bit of luck, a new future.

She didn't look back. Most the town watched her go. They didn't blame her. Some wished they'd had that kind of courage themselves.

Some thought staying – accepting – was also a form of courage.

No one else would leave. In a season, the only sound on the wind would be that of hinges and poorly secured screen doors. The only colors would be sand, dust, brick, and rust. Jill took the last of color with her.

The sun was cruel to her as she rode, but the road west was straight and clean. She went through her water too quickly, and she burned through her fuel; good fortune alone had put up a service station at the very edge of her bike's reach. It was, after a small bit of worry, perfect. She paid good money for the petrol, and even more for water, then continued westward. When she'd asked the gas jockey how much further to the next town, he mumbled something about moons, as though distance could be so measured.

Eventually, Jill was riding into the sunset.

After that, the long deserted road went dark. The heat of the day vanished like good intentions. She road on, into the night, with only her single headlamp and the moon providing any light. It was a grueling journey, far longer than any she'd ever undertaken. Her muscles ached, but the bike purred.

She rode more slowly in the night, but she didn't stop until she had no choice. She came off the road, propped her bike on its kickstand, and curled up within its slight shelter.

She slept thoroughly, albeit for only a short time, and woke as the sun began to peek over the eastern horizon.

With her shadow pointing the way, Jill passed road signs for places that no longer existed, billboards making promises they could no longer keep.

She reached the next service station and found the jockey there more willing to talk.

"Ain't seen no one on this road, weeks at a time," he said, "and now you show up so soon after the carnival."

She kept focused. "Did they say where they were going?"

He shook his head. "Can't say they did that, ma'am. But I reckon they'll be headed to the next town, just like they always do."

This gave Jill some hope.

Hours later, when her shadow was under her, Jill came to a crossroads. There was a working traffic light, though no traffic to control. She waited at the red anyhow and tried to decide which way they'd gone. Left, right, or straight ahead? She thought she maybe saw dust in the west, though it could be a storm or a mirage or a trick of the light.

When the signal changed to green, Jill pressed forward, westward, with as much speed as she dared. She reasoned that she, alone on a bike, could cover more distance than a collection of vehicles towing all the carnies and their equipment, the pieces used to put together their rides and midway, the fortune teller's props and the animals and the ticket booths.

And they must carry a good deal of food and, most importantly, water for these long treks between stops.

She reasoned rightly. When the sun set, she finally saw the caravan on the horizon, painted red and black and gold. This time, she didn't stop, and she didn't slow down.

She caught up to the Last Carnival's camp near midnight. The Ringmaster himself stood on the road, in the path of her headlamp's beam, as she approached.

He tipped his hat and said, "Welcome."

That was it. That was all that was needed. Inside the camp, cooks had made soup and bread; they refueled her bike and gave her water; and they gave her a job – which , although it's grueling and her muscles often ache, she performs even still.

ABOUT THE PROJECT AND AUTHOR

InkStains is a random collection of stories – fiction and nonfiction of any genre – handwritten daily over the course of a year.

This is the second series of InkStains.

John Urbancik is a writer and photographer currently residing in the Florida panhandle. He has lived in other places and is probably best known for his fantasy, dark fantasy, and horror stories and books.

An InkStains will be released at the beginning of every month to correspond with the months in which the stories were written. The author is completing a third series concurrently with the release of these. You can follow his journey on www.darkfluidity.com.

ALSO BY JOHN URBANCIK

NOVELS
Sins of Blood and Stone
Breath of the Moon
Once Upon a Time in Midnight
DarkWalker
Stale Reality
The Corpse and the Girl from Miami

NOVELLAS
A Game of Colors
The Rise and Fall of Babylon (with Brian Keene)
Wings of the Butterfly
House of Shadow and Ash
Necropolis
Quicksilver
Beneath Midnight
Zombies vs. Aliens vs. Robots vs. Cowboys vs. Ninja vs. Investment Bankers vs. Green Berets
Colette and the Tiger

COLLECTIONS
Shadows, Legends & Secrets
Sound and Vision
Tales of the Fantastic and the Phantasmagoric

INKSTAINS

STALE
REALITY

JOHN
URBANCIK

"What happens is, the world, everything we know,
this thing we call Reality, it exists in our heads.
It doesn't really exist. And someone decided they
didn't like Reality. Or maybe not that they didn't
like it, but they wanted to try another. They wanted
it so hard, Reality changed, and now we're in
their head. Not our own. See, their Reality shifted,
and in it, you don't exist. You just got left over."

Welcome to Kevin Nichols' new Reality.

PREVIEW

STALE REALITY

1.

I don't know *why* I'm here. I can tell you how. I can recall every step and every corner on the path from what had been my home to this—would you call it a *room?* Den, maybe, or cave, even a pit, but I don't think *room* is quite the right word.

The people here scare me. There's a guy using a knife—and I mean a *knife,* one designed to inflict serious damage—to clean his fingernails, and he won't stop looking at me. At least he doesn't stink as bad as some of the others. The stench is so thick, I nearly choked when I was brought here.

There's another guy, eyes steady as Mexican jumping beans, drool—or is that foam?—spilling from his mouth, a sheen of sweat and fresh blood on the side of his head. I don't think it's his blood.

The women are worse. One, a blonde with spikes in her knuckles, like claws, rusted or blood-stained or both, leans back all nonchalant, as if she's got no worries in a place like this. When I saw her, she met my eye and grinned. Her teeth have been filed into points.

I see at least three corpses—and smell them, they're not exactly fresh—but no one seems to care.

I'm half convinced this is Hell. I'm dead, and now I suffer.

There's a kid, can't be more than twelve, stepping across people scattered on the ground. He's dirty and scruffy, and he's not afraid. When one of the unmoving bodies suddenly reaches out and grasps him by the ankle, the kid whips out a switchblade and slashes the wrist. Not a word of warning. No reaction from anyone else, just a curse as the injured man yanks his hand back.

I can't stay here. There's no way. I can't live not knowing if my next breath may be my last.

I know. Real life was like that. you always had the possibility of getting struck down by an aneurism or an out of control truck or any random thing, but in real life Death doesn't stare at you, mocking and teasing, like it does here.

She said she'd take me to people like me, but I'm nothing like these people. Nothing. I'm not a killer.

"You don't look alright," a guy says to me. He's not the most unsavory here. His teeth look straight and clean and he doesn't contribute to the stench, but he's got a red scar on his unshaven cheek that looks fresh, his pupils are enormous, and every muscle seems to have a slight quiver.

I look around, hoping he's talking to someone else, but it's me. I'm not sure how to talk to these people. I don't want to betray my fear or show signs of weakness, but I don't really want to get into a conversation. I say, "Neither do you," and hope that'll be the end of it, that it's not too offensive or overly brotherly or anything other than enough to suggest I'm not stupid enough to ignore him.

He closes his eyes and lowers his head, shaking it, and says, "No, I guess I'm not, none of us is alright anymore. But you're new here."

It isn't a question, so I don't answer. He gives me a moment to respond anyhow, then continues. "Do you even know what's happened to you yet? Have you got any idea?"

"Actually," I tell him, "no."

"Oh, dude," he says, his eyes open again, looking like he's confiding something. "You've been totally fucked, is what. Same as everyone here. See, what happens is, the world, everything we know, this thing we call Reality, it exists in our heads. It doesn't really exist. It's what we make. I'm not real good at explaining things, but it's like this: someone decided they didn't like Reality. Or maybe not that they didn't like it, but they wanted to try another. They wanted it so hard, Reality changed, and now we're in their head instead. Not our own. See, their Reality shifted, and in it, you don't exist. None of us do. You shouldn't be here at all. You just got left over."

"Left over?"

"Reality, man, it's big. There's a lot of it. You try reshaping it, see if you don't forget a little something here, a little something there."

Now I'm really scared, because what he's saying almost makes sense. "If I'm not supposed to be here," I say, "then I never lived in my home."

"Ain't your home," he says. "Never was, except in your memory. But no one else is gonna remember that. No one else is gonna remember you."

I hope he's been taking something, some hardcore hallucinogen I've never heard of, some scary psychotica thing that warps the mind, because that'd be easier than if he's right.

But it matches what I've seen, what happened in my own home.

No—*not* my home, like he's telling me. Like the guy living there said before trying to put a bullet in my head.

9 novellas
8 vignettes
6 Nights of Midnight

TALES OF THE FANTASTIC
AND THE PHANTASMAGORIC

PREVIEW

MADMEN, POETS & THIEVES

Ah, but of course I remember the sun. I wasn't born in this horrible dark place, and believe me, I'll be elsewhere when I die. So yes, I remember the sun, and I remember sunrise over the ocean, so when a woman such as she walks into a room, wearing a dress the color of an ocean sunrise, with eyes like a twilight sky and hair like spider webs in moonlight—believe me, I know a mystery when I see one, and she, whoever she may be, whatever else she may claim, is one hundred percent mystery. I immediately know I must see her again, speak with her without restraint, unlock her passions and lose myself in her poisons. I'd known other women, a great many, I daresay, but the moment this mystery entered the room wearing an ocean sunrise, I forgot the names of all of them.

In fact, I can think of nothing and no one else, and can't recall why I'd been in the room in the first place, nor who else might be here. It could as easily have been a prison or a dancehall, though of course it's something bland, a restaurant, filled with a wait staff dressed quite casually. I should be surrounded by tuxedoes and capes and men with pocket watches, and certainly the woman wrapped in an ocean sunrise deserves nothing less. I gather my courage and wits from the darkest crevices within my very soul and, quite daringly, I stride across the big room and sit in the chair opposite her.

She sits alone. Such are the depths of her mystery, that she should ever be forced to dine alone except by choice. She looks at me with eyes like weapons and asks, "Do I know you?"

"Absolutely, I wish that was true," I say. "Would you allow me the chance to change the answer to an unambivalent yes?"

She does a great many things in response. She taps a perfectly painted fingernail on the edge of the table one time. Twice, she blinks, once perhaps to find meaning in my words and once more to find words to fit her meaning. She glances away, fleetingly, searching for some hidden camera or jokester or thief, but she cannot keep her eyes away.

I know it will be up to me to get this conversation started, so I say, "My name is Derek Smith, which may perhaps not sound like the most descriptive of names, except that I am, indeed, a smithy of a type. What would you prefer I call you?"

She graces me, then, with a smile, and says, "Angeline."

"Wonderful," I say. "I love a name with multiple syllables. You can change the meaning merely by adjusting your inflection and emphasis. Your mother, I believe, did you the greatest service by giving you such a wondrous name."

"You're trying my patience," she says.

Until that moment, I'd forgotten where we were. This is not my living room, or the concourse outside an opera house; this is a restaurant, and two waiters have arrived to take her order. More precisely, one has arrived to inquire if there was anything he could get her, and the other has come to be on hand should the thing she require be my removal.

"My apologies, then," I say, standing, still overcome by the ocean sunrise. "I must have mistaken you for a lover I lost in a dream." I do not, cannot, wait for a response. I flee. I go back to my table, where I take my coat and leave some coins, finish my whiskey in a single shot, and then, only after all that, I flee the restaurant.

Of course, I cannot go far. The gravity of the woman wrapped in an ocean sunrise is far too great a force to resist. I find a place to stand, where I can support my shoulders against bricks older than my bones, and think about the great poems I will write as I uncover each layer of mystery. I look up to the moon and implore her, the goddess within her or the very rock in the sky, I know not. I beg for the right words. I fear I may have already blundered, or at least put myself at a great disadvantage. I must learn to pace myself, or to think before I act, but then I wouldn't be who I am and what would be the fun in that?

Time means nothing to me. It flows and ebbs and turns back upon itself at its whim, not mine. In this City of Night, it is always nighttime, even when it is noon, so you cannot convince me to trust in a clock or a watch or a timekeeper of any sort. When the appointed hour arrives, you might say, the mystery wrapped in an ocean sunrise emerges from the restaurant, sees me in my spot across the street, and strides straight toward me. She smiles, but not in some grandiose way; it's without promise or conviction. When she's still several paces away but has captured my gaze, she says, "You waited for me." It isn't a question, so I give no answer. "You're mad."

"I might be," I admit, "but I blame you."

"You don't know the first thing about me," she says.

"I know your mother named you Angeline," I says. "I know you dined alone, though I cannot fathom why. I could have sat across from you and admired you from close up, rather than from afar."

She looks over her shoulder. "You can't see inside the restaurant from here," she says.

"But I see the memory of you perfectly fine," I say, tapping my head beside my eye. "Isn't that worth something?"

"No," she says.

"It's worth something to me," I tell her.

"You're wrong," she says. "It's nothing. It's less than nothing. It's *sad*, is what it is."

"Sad, then," I say, "is still more than nothing."

"Have you got any money?" she asks.

"As much as I need."

"Excellent," she says. "Buy me a drink."

Coming in 2017:

The Corpse and the Girl from Miami

THE CORPSE
AND THE GIRL FROM MIAMI

PREVIEW

He wakes atop a fresh grave. He's muddy and achy, and he can barely see through the gloom. Fortunately, there's the near constant flicker of lightning, and a continuous roll of thunder with violent punctuations. The flashes are blinding. The rain feels like bullets. He knows what bullets feel like. He's cold, and he's stiff, and he's not exactly sure how he got here.

Between lightning strikes, he reads the tombstone: Armando Luis Salazar. Name means nothing to him. But since he doesn't remember his own, that's no surprise.

Faces watch him from the shadows, hiding behind the trees and mausoleums and gravestones, some closer than others, but there's nothing real out there, nothing substantial. These are ghosts, mere echoes of memories. He approaches one; it fades, and others appear in alternative hidey holes, behind other stones, on the other side of the iron fence.

The rain has soaked him thoroughly. His clothes, torn and dirty, are a total loss. No shoes. Wallet, yes. Inside, he finds money – not much, and no pictures – credit cards and a license all in the name of Armando Luis Salazar.

He knows that's not him.

He also knows he's no grave robber.

The license offers his only clue: an address in Boston.

He knows the streets well enough. He finds his way rather easily. Too easily, he thinks. Something's amiss, but he's not sure what.

The license leads him to an old three decker between a dozen others. It stands three stories, sports a steep roof, gutters overflowing with rainwater, two windows on the ground and second level, one at the top. Light seeps around the drapes of one of the second floor windows. The porch, though small, is the first relief he's had from the rain.

Besides the wallet, he'd found nothing in his pockets. He feels the jamb above the door and is rewarded with a shiny silver key. It opens the door.

The foyer is small, dark, and claustrophobically filled. Coat rack, chair, semi-circle table against the wall, oversized plant and a book on it; stairs straight up, doors on either side, one straight ahead; an umbrella stand, even a tiny mirror beside the door with three pegs for keys. A set hangs from only one.

He doesn't bother with the doors. One will be a closet; it's too close to the house next door. The others will lead to kitchen and living room, but not to answers. He leaves a trail of watery steps up the wood stairs.

At the landing, a short hall leads to the front. There's a door right here, closed, two more leading to rooms with windows facing the street, and a bathroom halfway down the hall.

Cautiously, he pushes open the door on his left and enters the room with the light. It comes from a single lamp between the window and a reading chair. Pictures hang on the walls and stand on the table. There's no bed here, but a series of books on built-in shelves. There's a closet with sliding doors. Heavy drapes over the window.

It takes all of two seconds to see there's nothing to be seen, but it's too long. He feels a sharp jab in his kidney, the cold barrel of a pistol. A woman's voice whispers a question: "Who are you?"

He hasn't tried his voice. It's dusty, despite the rain. "I don't know."

"What do you mean, you don't know?"

His hands are up, and if he moves them he'll catch a bullet. He says, "Wallet."

She reaches into his back pocket, extracts the leather so expertly he barely feels it. She flips it open, pushes the gun deeper into his back. "Armando Luis Salazar," she says. "He's dead."

"So I gathered."

"In the room, in the chair, let me look at you." She shoves with the gun, as though he didn't know which of the single chair in the room he was meant to choose. He walks slowly, but doesn't have enough pieces to put anything together. When he reaches the chair, he turns and he sits.

She's still at the doorway. Gun pointed directly at him. She wears jeans, a tee shirt, nothing special or overt, but she's sexy as hell. He doesn't remember any other woman at all. Short dark hair, gleaming eyes – maybe green, maybe blue, hard to tell with so little light.

She throws the wallet back at him. He catches it, but makes no other move. The gun's still aimed, and though the rest of her is calm and cool and collected, her finger looks twitchy. Maybe it's just unused to the weapon. He's fairly sure he's had guns pointed at him before.

"Who are you?" she asks again.

"Gave you all I got," he says.

"What the hell does that mean?"

"Means I'm not sure. I don't know. I don't remember."

She grins. It's a grin that says she doesn't believe him. "What do you remember, smartass?"

"I remember waking up in the cemetery in the rain."

"Yeah, you and everyone else. We've all done that. What else?" Strange thing for her to say; he's fairly certain that particular memory is rather unique.

"I had his wallet. So I came here."

"You're a fool."

"I imagine I ain't the only one."

"You're also stupid," she says. She's relaxed, but she hasn't lowered the gun, won't lower it, can't completely trust him. "You hungry? Thirsty? Tired?" She's asking as though she might care, but she doesn't, she can't, and it makes him uneasy. The answers shouldn't be what most people would answer.

So he tells her, "I ache." He does. Every muscle. As though he'd been beaten with baseball bats. No bones broken, no lacerations – at least, none he's aware of – but stiff and somewhat tired.

"You're a mess," she tells him.

And he tells her, "You were expecting me." No question. A statement of fact. He'd not made enough noise to alert her. Didn't even squish when he walked. How long had she been sitting in the dark, waiting?

"Of course we were," another voice says. Behind her: a man, older, fit and broad, with goatee and an ingratiating smile that will completely annoy anyone within three minutes. Salesman, except in a better suit, with an unnatural twinkle in his left eye, as though that particular eye was the only one that mattered. He steps in past the woman. "And she should've introduced herself. This is Ofelia. She knew, what did you call him? Salazar."

"And you?"

"Gerald. Gerald Maker. It's Welsh, the name, and very old. Older than I am. The real question tonight, my boy, is what do we call you?"

He's crossed half the room before stopping. He swings his hands when he speaks, wide sweeps, thick expressive fingers. Ofelia hasn't moved, hasn't lowered the gun, though her eyes have shifted to Mr. Maker. He bends over, looking more closely at the man in the pistol's firing zone. "You are something of an amazement, even I must admit that. You say you remember nothing?"

"Do I know you?"

"No, my boy," Mr. Maker says. "It was Ofelia who called me in. You weren't here."

"Where was I?"

"Would you believe me if I said you were dead?"

"No."

"Well, perhaps you should."

"No." The simple denial seems untruthful and misleading. There's no vehemence behind it, no emotion at all, and he wonders if his forgotten name is, in fact, Armando Luis Salazar. He wonders, but doubts it. He decides he can't believe anything Mr. Maker says.

"Anyhow." Mr. Maker turns to Ofelia, though he's still close enough to be grabbed, punched, kicked, strangled, whatever. Mr. Maker's not worried; she's still got the gun trained on the chair, and he's walking past her to get out of the room. "I believe I've proven my worth, Ms. Ofelia. Shall we get on to the real thing?"

She says, "Yes."

As he disappears into the gloom behind her, he says, "Then take care of him. Don't worry. There'll be little blood."

She hesitates, only briefly; then it's three shots, a triangle in the chest. He looks down at the wounds. Mr. Maker was right, there's no blood. He tries to stand, but his legs falter and he drops noisily to the floor. He's still covered by aches, but the bullets holes hurt like lava.

She's already turning away. "I didn't doubt you, Mr. Maker. But it is extraordinary."

"No worries, my dear," he's saying, but he's almost too far away to hear. "Corpse-raising isn't exactly a widely practiced art."

Ofelia's walking away. The burning bullets are melting into the other aches that cover him. He knows his name wasn't Armando Luis Salazar, but he doesn't know what it was. He was practice. The real thing, presumably Salazar, is next. But there's a problem.

He needs to use the chair to support himself, but he manages to stand. His legs are weak, but not dead weight. There's no blood. And, to be perfectly honest, getting shot now didn't hurt near as much as when he'd been alive. And since he's not alive, not really, since he suddenly realizes he's not been breathing, he's merely a collection of over-stimulated nerve endings, three bullets or a hundred wouldn't make him dead again.

He peeks out the window. They're walking through the rain toward the cemetery. That's okay. He can wait. When they get back, he'll be waiting in the dark. And while he may have no gun, and his strength isn't what it was, that's okay, too. There's a kitchen downstairs. He'll find a knife.

COMING IN 2017